JULIE
and the kitten

Illustrations by José-Luis Macias S.
Original story by J. Barnabé Dauvister
Retold by Jane Carruth

Muffin and Julie suddenly hear a noise
in the attic. "Who can it be?" they ask
each other, a little worried.

What a surprise, it's a kitten!
But however did she get there? Imagine finding a kitten
among the old treasures in the attic!

Poor little kitten! What are you doing here all alone? Well, now you are among friends. Don't worry. I'll take care of you!

Muffin and I will teach you to play with a ball. My homework and lessons can easily wait for a bit.

Wednesday: it's time to get the tea ready. Lucy, Charlotte and Sophie will be here soon. Come on Muffin, and you too, Kitty, help me finish this cake. We must be quick.

Julie's three friends are here already. They want to see who can paint the best picture of Muffin. But where has Kitty gone? Ding dong, ding dong! "Come quickly! Tea's ready!" Julie cries, shaking her little bell.

Oh no! Lucy, Sophie, Charlotte and Julie can't believe their eyes! So that's where that rascal Kitty has been! She went looking for her six little brothers so they can enjoy Julie's delicious tea too.

With a hop and a scamper all the kittens run away. The little girls aren't quick enough to catch them.

Don't run off, kittens! Don't be afraid! We're not cross with you. We know you must be hungry!

Please come out of your hiding-places, kittens. Don't be so frightened. We have fresh milk here for you. Here they come! Now we can all be good friends. Aren't they sweet?

Julie's attic now has seven new tenants. She brings them a big jug of milk every day. Thanks to her the kittens will grow up fast — so all the mice in the house had better watch out!

Published in the United States and simultaneously in Canada by Joshua Morris, Inc
431 Post Road East, Westport, CT 0688(
Printed in Belgiun